Gracie's Passover Surprise

"*When things go wrong, we can surely depend
on our loved ones—our family and wonderful friends.*"
—Papa

D1598030

For David, Tara, Brett, Brooke & Ryan.
You make my heart sing.
And for Nadine, who loved Passover.
—L.T.G.

LYNN TAYLOR GORDON is delighted to introduce *Gracie's Passover Surprise*,
the second offering from the award-winning Gracie series. Lynn lives in southern New Jersey
with her husband, David, and loves spending time with her family and fur babies.

LAURA BROWN is an illustrator and designer who lives in Richmond, Virginia.

Thank You!
Bonnie Feingold Gremont: Your wonderful imagination and fun family dinners inspired this story.
Pashko family: Your love, support, and knowledge of all things Passover were invaluable in the
writing of this story.

Stephanie Bart-Horvath, art director/designer, and Janet Frick, line and copy editor:
Thank you for your kindness, insight, creativity, expertise, and friendship.
Like Gracie and Papa, we make a great team!

Gracie's Passover Surprise
Copyright © 2019 by Lynn Taylor Gordon
Printed in Canada.
Library of Congress Control Number: 2018961734   ISBN 978-0-9857353-3-3
First Edition

To contact the author, request a reading, or obtain permission to use a quote from this book,
please visit cookieandnudgebooks.com

Gracie's Passover Surprise

by Lynn Taylor Gordon
illustrated by Laura Brown

COOKIE & NUDGE books

GRACIE HOPPED OUT OF BED with soft, sleepy-time hair,
swept open her window, and felt the cool air.
A mama bird perched on the tree branch next door
and fed worms to her babies—Grace counted four.

In the kitchen, sheer curtains puffed out on the breeze.
Papa reached for his hankie and muffled a sneeze.
"Oh, Papa, it's spring!" Gracie sang with a smile.
"That means Passover's coming in just a short while!"
"You're right," replied Papa, while toasting his bread.
"Soon we'll be munching on matzo instead."

"And, Papa," coaxed Gracie, "remember last year,
when you said that we'd host this Passover here?"
"I do," replied Papa. "I'll make all the calls.
You'll be up to your elbows in matzo balls!"

Grace pulled a stool to a tall, dusty nook
and wobbled a bit as she tugged down a book.

The old cookbook's pages were yellowed and worn,
with thumbprints in margins; some pages were torn.
She found notes from the cook—more of this, less of that—
and a few surprise photos, all faded and flat.

One beautiful print that she plucked from the pile
was a picture of Mama with her special smile.
These were *her* thumbprints; *she* was the cook.
These were *her* recipes; this was *her* book.

Max gave a yawn, then got up from his nap
and laid his big head down upon Gracie's lap.
Gracie gave him a hug and a kiss on his head.
"We'll make all her favorites," Grace softly said.

"Gracie," said Papa, "we must make a list
of the chores to be done, so that none will be missed.
There's cleaning and shopping and cooking and baking.
This Seder of ours will be some undertaking!"
"You're right, Pop," said Gracie. "Let's start right away.
It's time to get ready for our special day!"

FOLD LAUNDRY

MAKE MATZO BALLS

BATHE PETS

WASH DISHES

TIDY BEDROOM

MOP

With dust cloths and brooms,
they cleaned cabinets and floors,
sweeping corner to corner, and
under the doors.

Next, under the sofa,
the beds and the vents . . .
Then they sold all the chametz for
twenty-five cents.

Soon Max and Bagel went into the tub,
and Papa gave Lox's glass fishbowl a scrub.
It sure wasn't easy, but when they were through,
Max, Lox, and Bagel looked almost brand-new.

Gracie set up the tables in three crooked rows.
Some tables were high, and others were low.
Each table was covered with cream-colored lace,
with Haggadahs and kippahs set neatly in place.
Then she added one cup, and placed it with care
for the Prophet Elijah, who just might be there.

Papa startled awake at the first light of dawn
to find Grace hard at work with her apron tied on.
"Oy vey!" exclaimed Papa. "It's Hurricane Grace!"
There were bowls, pots, and pans all over the place.
"Ha!" Papa laughed. "I was right after all:
you *are* up to your elbows in matzo balls!"

Then Grace replied, "Pop, it's all under control.
Please rinse off this pot and then hand me that bowl.
And please, Papa dear, help me wipe up this mess.
Oh, thank you," she added. "Hey, Pop, you're the best!"
"Gracie," said Papa, "we make a great team.
You make the mess and then *I* make it clean!"

Grace followed each recipe, read every label,
then set all the food on their small kitchen table:
gefilte fish, brisket, and latkes still steaming.
As Papa watched Gracie, his whole face was beaming.

Then Papa saw Grace make a dash for the door.
"Just remembered an item we missed at the store.
The haroset needs walnuts! I called Mrs. G.—
she said to run up, and she'll share hers with me."

So Gracie dashed up to the next-higher floor,
where Mrs. G. called out, "Don't stand in the door!"

"Come in. Have a seat. Have a drink. Want a nosh?"
"I'd love to," said Grace, "but I'm in such a rush."

Mrs. G. gave a sigh and then tilted her head.
"Now, where did I put all the walnuts?" she said.
"Grace, you're making Pesach! So much you'll be learning. . . ."
Then she suddenly sniffed. "I smell something burning!"

"Me, too!" shouted Gracie. "I really must run,
with so much on my list—so much to be done.
Thanks for the walnuts. Will I see you later?"
"With bells on, dear Gracie. Would I miss your Seder?"

Then Grace sprinted downstairs from Mrs. G.'s floor,
to find Papa pacing outside of their door.
"Gracie," gasped Papa, "while you were gone,
I fell fast asleep with the oven still on.
Everyone's fine, so please don't you fret.
This is all my fault. Oh, don't be upset."

"Mama's kugel is ruined! Oh no," wailed poor Grace.
Then, "How did this food get all over the place?"
Papa looked thoughtful and then scratched his head.

"Well, I'm no detective," he finally said,
"but I think our suspects are under the table:
they're Briskethead Max and his best buddy, Bagel."

He held Gracie's face as he wiped off her tears.
"You'll make Mama's favorites again, Grace—next year.
Just look at the brisket on old Max's head.
Sometimes you just have to laugh," Papa said.

Then Gracie *was* laughing, and Papa laughed too.
Together they cleaned up, and soon they were through.
As they mopped up the last of the food on the floor,
there came a soft tapping sound at their front door.

"They're here," whispered Papa. "Uh-oh!" Gracie said.
"I'm all covered in schmutz, from my feet to my head.
I'm still in my jammies, Pop—what will they think?"
"Don't you worry one bit," he replied with a wink.

Gracie looked through the peephole, rubbing her eyes,
and felt her cheeks blush when she saw the surprise.
Right there in the hallway, lined up two by two,
stood her family and friends, wearing *their* pj's, too!

Dressed in cotton and satin, with robes to the floor,
some wore fun, fuzzy slippers in colors galore.
Gracie greeted each guest with a kiss and a smile,
complimenting them all on their Passover style.

They marched through the doorway with pots, pans, and chairs,
plus some brown shopping bags stuffed with Passover fare:
chicken soup, matzo balls, brisket, and more
were lovingly carried through Gracie's front door.

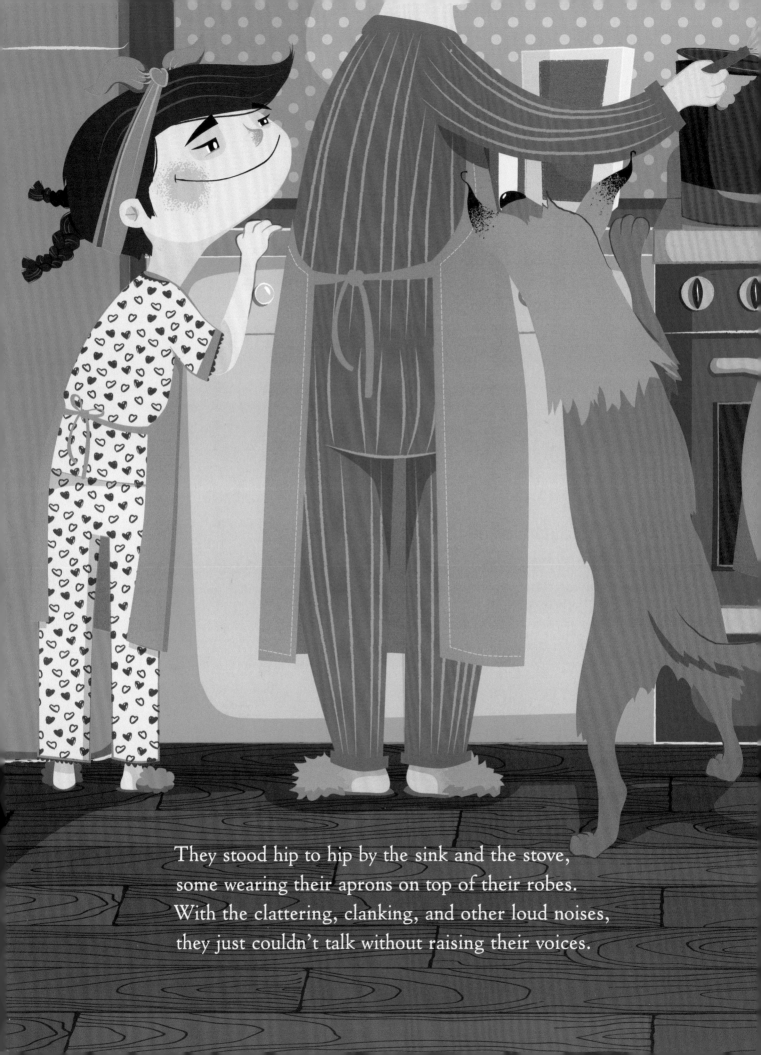

They stood hip to hip by the sink and the stove,
some wearing their aprons on top of their robes.
With the clattering, clanking, and other loud noises,
they just couldn't talk without raising their voices.

"Oy, my back is so achy." "My shoulders are sore."
"You call that knee swollen? Well, mine's swollen more!"
Grace quietly watched as they all worked together,
then suddenly found herself feeling much better.

Papa said Kiddush, then nodded his head.
"Tonight I am feeling so thankful," he said,
"for this honored tradition that's centuries old,
where our story of freedom is once again told."

Then Papa gave Gracie a quick little wink.
"Now, my sweet girl, here's what I truly think.
Sometimes in our lives we cannot understand
why our very best efforts don't work out as planned.
But when things go wrong, we can surely depend
on our loved ones—our family and wonderful friends."

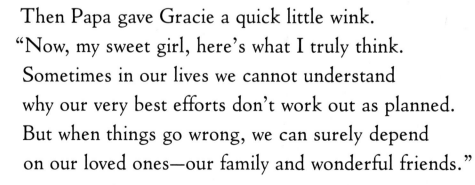

Papa reached for the matzo in everyone's view,
took the middle piece out, and then broke it in two.
When no one was watching, he wrapped it with care,
then hid the afikomen beneath Gracie's chair.

Gracie looked out at the three crooked rows
of the tables she'd set only one day ago.
Mama's fine Seder plate shone in its place,
and Gracie was thankful for each caring face.

"Thank you," she said, with a gleam in her eyes,
"for this wonderful, cozy Passover surprise!
And, if you don't mind, I have one small addition:
pj's at Passover—our *new* tradition!"

The years have flown by, and now Gracie is grown,
with a wonderful family and home of her own.
Her mama's old cookbook is even more worn,
with more thumbprints in margins and more pages torn.
But the memory it brings will always burn bright:
how a family tradition was started that night.

Gracie's Glossary*

afikomen *(ah-fee-KOH-muhn)*: A piece of matzo is broken in two. The larger piece becomes the afikomen, and is then hidden. The finder, usually the youngest child, receives a small prize.

chametz *(HAH-metz)*: Any food (such as bread) that is made of grain and water and has been allowed to rise. Prior to Passover, we clear our homes of chametz for a short time.

Haggadah *(huh-GAH-duh)*: A very old Jewish book that sets the order of a Passover Seder, including prayers, blessings, rituals, and songs. The word "Haggadah" means "telling" in Hebrew.

haroset *(ha-RO-set)*: A special mixture of chopped apples, nuts, and sweet wine.

Kiddush *(KID-ush)*: The blessing said over the wine.

kippah *(KIH-pa)*: A head covering worn while praying. Also known as a yarmulke.

matzo *(MAHT-suh)*: A square, flat cracker with a slightly wavy surface. The Israelites were in such a hurry to leave Egypt, there was no time for their dough to rise, and they were forced to eat unleavened bread, matzo. During Passover, we eat matzo to remind us of this journey.

Pesach *(PAY-sak)*: Hebrew term for Passover. A time of celebration and reflection marking the Israelites' exodus from slavery in Egypt about 3000 years ago.

Prophet Elijah, the *(PROF-it ih-LIE-juh, the)*: A Hebrew prophet who lived many thousands of years ago. We await his arrival at Passover by keeping the door ajar as a sign of welcome, and we prepare the Cup of Elijah, which is the fifth ceremonial cup of wine.

Seder plate *(SAY-der plate)*: A plate appointed to hold symbolic items that remind us of the Israelites' struggle to reach freedom: the shankbone (zeroa), egg (beitzah), bitter herbs (maror), vegetable (karpas), and a sweet paste (haroset).

*Because many of the terms in this glossary are taken from Hebrew or Yiddish, some have more than one English spelling or pronunciation. Please note that different Jewish communities—and even families within communities—have their own Passover traditions.